HEATHER AT THE BARRE

by Sheri Cooper Simkin

A

Illustrations by
Richard Lauter and Ed Tadiello

Spot Illustrations by
Rich Grote

MagicAttic Club

For more information contact:
Book Editor, Magic Attic Press, 866 Spring Street,
P.O. Box 9722, Portland, ME 04104-5022

First Edition
Printed in the United States of America
3 4 5 6 7 8 9 10

Magic Attic Club is a registered trademark.

Betsy Gould, Publisher
Marva Martin, Art Director
Robin Haywood, Managing Editor

Edited by Judit Bodnar
Designed by Susi Oberhelman

ISBN 157513-007-6

Magic Attic Club books are printed on acid-free, recycled paper.

As members of the
MAGIC ATTIC CLUB,
we promise to
be best friends,
share all of our adventures in the attic,
use our imaginations,
have lots of fun together,
and remember—the real magic is in us.

Alison   *Keisha*

Heather   *Megan*

Contents

Chapter

One

A SURPRISE FROM AUNT JANTINA

he newspaper's entertainment section stretched before Heather on the living room floor. She pressed the soles of her feet together and let her knees flop outward like a frog's. To her dismay, they didn't flop all that far.

"Mom," she called up through the air vent that led to her mother's art studio, "Aunt Jantina's coming to town! She's doing *The Sleeping Beauty*. Isn't that great?"

Footsteps padded overhead. Moments later Heather's

mom appeared on the stairway. Her hands glistened with wet clay.

"Did you hear what I said?"

Mrs. Hardin nodded. "It's fantastic. Imagine her still dancing at my age! Last I heard, she was going to retire."

"Lucky for us, she didn't." Heather grinned. "We do get to go, don't we?"

The doorbell chimed then, and Mom wiggled her gray fingers at Heather. "Get that, honey, will you?"

"Okay. It's probably for me anyway." Alison, Megan, and Keisha were coming over to make plans for their last day of winter vacation. Ever since they'd discovered the attic in their neighbor's house and formed the Magic Attic Club, the girls had been inseparable.

Heather swung the door wide, letting in a blast of wintry air. She was surprised when a delivery man handed her a cardboard envelope and asked her to sign on line twenty-three.

"Go ahead and open it," her mother called from the stairs. She had an I-know-something-you-don't-know tone in her voice.

Heather unzipped the easy-open strip and pulled out what appeared to be four tickets clipped to a handwritten note with JANTINA FERRIS embossed in gold. "Mom, look! She sent us tickets!" Waving them in the air, Heather danced toward the stairs, ending in a stiff *grand jeté* leap.

Her mom laughed. "I think we'd better find you a new dance school, before you hurt yourself."

Heather's lips twitched at the insult. She knew enough—the French names of all the steps and how she was supposed to do them. Could she help it if her body wouldn't cooperate? "I'm just rusty," she said.

"You certainly are," her mom agreed. "Still, it does no good to practice the wrong way. Ask Jantina."

"I will." Heather bit back a pout.

Mrs. Hardin went back upstairs to her pottery wheel. Heather laid the tickets on the coffee table and sat down to await her friends. Assuming the frog position again, she leaned hard on her knees in frustration. Why couldn't her legs cooperate and lie flat on the floor the way a good dancer's were supposed to?

At last the bell rang again. Heather pushed away all thoughts of dancing and rushed to open the door.

Alison stood in front of Megan and Keisha, bearing a steaming pie on outstretched hands. "Look what I made, and it's all for us."

"Mmmm. Smells good," said Heather. "Come on in. Warm up!" The sweet nip of cinnamon soon filled the entry hall as Alison and the others took their coats off and tossed them on the brass rack. "I've got the most exciting news to tell you!"

"What?" asked Keisha. "Did you go through the mirror again?"

Heather shook her head.

"Then what is it?" Keisha's dark eyes glowed with anticipation. "No secrets, Heather. Not from *us*!"

Heather sat Alison's pie on the coffee table, right next to Jantina's ballet tickets. She noticed that Megan was already reading the fine print, even though they were upside down.

Megan giggled when Heather caught her eye. "Sorry, I can't help it."

"No kidding," Alison teased. "She'd read the phone book if she really got hard up."

Megan blushed. "So? What's the surprise?"

"We're going to see *The Sleeping Beauty*! One of my mom's best friends is dancing Princess Aurora and she sent us four tickets."

"We? You mean, us?" Megan pressed her hands together beneath her chin and let loose a little squeal. "I've always wanted to go to a ballet."

"Me, too," Keisha chimed in. "Oh, Heather, this is going to be cool!"

Alison only shrugged. "Maybe I'll like it. Who knows?"

"You'll *love* it," said Megan. "This is going to be the best thing we've ever done together. Outside of the attic, of course."

A lump settled in the back of Heather's throat and wouldn't budge. There was no way she could ask her family not to go. Still, the other girls sounded like they were already counting on the four of them going together. "Well, um . . . these *might* be for my family," hedged Heather at last. "I'm not sure. I'll have to check. But I just *know* Aunt Jantina can get three more. All I have to do is ask her. Like I said, she's a star."

"And you really know her, right?" Megan asked.

She doesn't believe me, Heather thought, wounded by Megan's tone. "Know her?" she blurted. "I'm like part of her family. She'd do anything for me. Really. Matter of fact, she even taught me how to dance. Said I could make it as a real ballerina, if I wanted to." That wasn't exactly the truth, but what could a little white lie hurt?

"Wow!" Keisha looked impressed. "I didn't know you could dance, Heather."

"It's been awhile, but I know what I need to do," Heather said firmly. "I just need to practice is all."

"Are you on toe yet?" asked Alison.

"Oh sure. It's fun. That's the best part."

"That's funny. *Dancer* magazine said you should be twelve to be on toe," Megan said gently.

Megan and her reading! Heather fumed inwardly. "I'm advanced, that's all," she said, dismissing her friend's concern. But she couldn't miss the look that passed between Megan, Alison, and Keisha.

"So call that Jantina lady, okay?" Keisha urged, and turned to the others. "It's lucky for us Heather has such great connections, isn't it?"

Megan nodded emphatically. Alison nodded, too, with less enthusiasm. But Alison would see how great ballet was. How could she know whether she'd like it, if she hadn't ever seen it? Heather reached for Aunt Jantina's letter, then for the phone.

Chapter Two

WHISPERS
AND LIES

When Aunt Jantina
answered sleepily,
Heather looked at her watch, worried
that she'd called too early. But it was almost ten.
"I—I'm sorry," she stammered. "I didn't mean to wake
you. It's me, Heather. No, Heather *Hardin*."

"Did the tickets arrive yet?"

"Yes, thank you. I'm so excited, which is why I was
wondering—"

"Shoot, it's late. I'm glad you woke me. I've got to take class at eleven."

"You still take classes?" Heather's voice climbed in surprise and dismay. She turned her back on her friends to hide her reaction. Surely the great Jantina Ferris didn't have to take classes anymore. She was the star.

"We *all* take classes, love. One a day keeps old age at bay." Aunt Jantina laughed lightly. "Like vitamins, eh?"

"I—I guess so." She glanced over her shoulder, wishing she could tell what Megan, Keisha, and Alison were thinking. But their faces were as closed as books.

"So, what's up, love? Is your mom okay?"

"She's fine. The reason I'm calling is, I told my friends you could get three more tickets. You know, so they could come with us opening night."

"Shoot, I wish I could. But it's a sellout. Not a seat to be had anywhere—not even in the nose-bleed section."

"Oh, no." Heather pressed her lips together.

"Sorry, Heather. Maybe next time. Listen, I've got to scoot. See you soon, okay? Kiss, kiss."

"Kiss, kiss," repeated Heather slowly, with disappointment.

Keisha rushed forward. "Is she all right? She didn't pull a muscle or anything, did she?"

"No, she's okay." Heather decided not to tell them the

part about Aunt Jantina's needing to take a class. Then they'd really wonder how good she was. Better to cut straight to the bad news. Heather sighed. "I guess I spoke too soon, though. She can't get more tickets. Says it's a sellout."

Megan's lips twitched. "I thought you said she was the star. . . ."

"Big deal," Alison said. "So we don't go to a dumb old ballet."

"It's not dumb and that's not the point," replied Megan patiently. "Heather said—"

"She *is* the star. Look at the ad." Heather swept the newspaper off the floor and waved it at Megan. "See? With Jantina Ferris, Renée Dobson and Marco Galicia."

Megan read it quickly, then passed it back. "*Three* stars? I don't think so."

"Megan," said Keisha gently.

"Well, I'm sorry. She doesn't have to lie. Not to us." Megan looked tough, with her arms crossed that way, but her eyes seemed to beg Heather to be honest.

"Who's to say she's lying?" Alison cut in. "She knows more about ballet than the rest of us put together. You've been taking lessons for years, right, Heather?"

Heather nodded. "And I've had four—no, five— different teachers, too."

"But that's not *your* fault," Keisha said, as if having lots of teachers were a bad thing. "You've moved a lot, that's all."

"Look, I know what I read," Megan replied firmly, "and books and things don't lie."

It was that bit about being on toe again. Heather's stomach went tight, as if Megan had just punched her. She hadn't lied, exactly. But it seemed that each exaggeration sparked another one, and it was getting hard to keep her story straight.

"Just forget it," Alison said. "Let's decide what we're going to do before we waste the whole day."

"We could eat your pie," Keisha suggested, "even if it is before lunch." She grinned mischievously.

Heather jumped at the chance to escape Megan's gaze. "I'll get the plates." Why couldn't Megan just let it go, like Alison said?

Heather's older sister, Jenna, was slouched over the kitchen table, working a crossword puzzle and picking at a bran muffin. She looked up when Heather began banging drawers closed in search of a spatula. "What's the matter with you?"

Heather could hear soft voices from the dining room. They were talking about her. She just knew it. If only she could hear what they were saying!

"Heather," Jenna persisted, "what's wrong?"

"They think I'm lying about Aunt Jantina," Heather whispered, "that she's not a star. I said she could get tickets, and she can't and maybe . . . maybe she's not such a big deal dancer anymore. I mean, she's as old as Mom, you know?"

Jenna's dimple deepened, the way it always did when she was trying not to smile.

"It's not funny, Jen. They're in there right now, saying what a liar I am. I just know it. All on account of some Renée lady being listed in the ad, too." Heather pulled four clean plates and forks from the dishwasher as quietly as she could, still hoping to catch some of her friends' words. She had thought, after they found the golden key and formed the Magic Attic Club, that they accepted her into their group. Now, she wondered. Would these nagging new-kid doubts ever go away?

"They don't know the roles, that's all," said Jenna. "Aunt Jantina's Princess Aurora. *She's* the one who dances with Prince Désiré."

"Marco Galicia," Heather cut in, and Jenna's eyes went dreamy at the mention of his name.

"Anyway, that other dancer—what's-her-name?— she's the Lilac Fairy. Just go on in there and explain it. They'll understand."

19

Heather nodded, wishing she could admit to Jenna how she'd stretched the truth about her own dancing ability. Now the memory of her words made her cheeks go hot with embarrassment. What had made her say such things?

The girls' whispering stopped when Heather entered the dining room. She plastered on a smile and managed to serve up Alison's apple pie, all the while dreading what would happen next. Somehow she wasn't surprised when Megan, Alison, and Keisha each had very convincing reasons for going home right after they'd eaten.

Chapter

Three

HEATHER
ON TOE

eather watched her friends hurry down the front walk, cross the street, and head for Alison's. The girls had hung out at the McCanns' together for years, Heather reminded herself. Why *wouldn't* they go there?

The old white Victorian house next door to Alison's caught her attention. The owner, a music and drama teacher named Ellie Goodwin, had been her mom's voice teacher when she was a girl. Back in the neighborhood after several years abroad, Ellie had given the girls a standing invitation to visit her attic. Heather couldn't think of a better time to go there than right now.

"Jenna," she called, "tell Mom I've gone to Ellie's, okay? I'll be back in awhile."

"Okay. See you later."

Heather bundled up and headed over to her neighbor's. She tried not to think about what was going on inside Alison's. Surely nothing as wonderful as what awaited her in Ellie's attic! When she rang the bell, Ellie responded by tapping on the parlor window and waving. Heather turned and smiled at the sight of the intriguing older woman.

Today she wore an exotic, animal-print silk scarf bib-fashion over a black dress. Dangly earrings danced as she motioned for Heather to come in. "I have a student now," she mouthed, and Heather nodded.

The heavy front door groaned as Heather opened it and slipped inside. Sandalwood incense snaked through the house, along with the sound of tentative piano playing. Heather hung her parka in the closet. Then she collected the key to the

attic from a silver box on the
table in the entry hall and
went upstairs.

As she turned the key in
the lock, her heart raced with
anticipation. The ballet tutu! That's
what she would try on this time. She
clattered up the attic stairs and pulled the tasseled cord
on the hanging lamp. A warm blush filled the room.

Heather hurried to open the huge steamer trunk and
quickly rummaged through the colorful outfits inside.
The pink tutu, with its stiff layers of netting, practically
sprang to the surface. She whisked it high into the
air and spun about, hugging the tutu to her chest.

"I'll bet this is just like Aunt Jantina's!" Heather
whispered in awe. The memory of the girls' first adventure
in the attic flooded back. She couldn't imagine where her
adventure might take her—and she could hardly wait to
find out. "Now for the toe shoes!"

Laying the outfit on the crimson oriental carpet,
she hurried to the massive mahogany wardrobe and
searched among Ellie's collection of hats, photographs,
diaries, and stage props. At last, she found the pale
pink toe shoes with satin ribbons nestled beside a
jeweled handbag.

Hurriedly, she cast her own shoes aside and put the dancing slippers on. Scooting off the rug, she stood up hesitantly on the hardwood floor. It felt just like the ones in all those dance studios across the country where she'd taken a few months of lessons and then moved on.

Dance-running across the expanse, she stretched her arms out in first . . . no . . . second . . . position. But the horrible thundering of the stiff, wooden toe boxes brought her up short. Surely Aunt Jantina didn't thump like a herd of elephants. What was the secret?

Maybe the mirror would show her. What had Ellie told them the first time they'd played in the attic? "You need the mirror, of course, but the real magic's in you."

Heather laughed. "Magic in me? She's got to be kidding."

Still, she retrieved the exquisite tutu from the rug and tried it on, shivering in the old attic. "Well, here goes," she whispered as she approached the tall, gilded mirror beside the wardrobe.

Sunlight sliced through the high dormer windows, bouncing off the mirror and about the room as specks of rainbow. Heather alternately grinned and squinted at the reflection of the dark-haired ballerina who smiled back at her and seemed to shiver, too.

Closing her eyes for a moment, she felt butterfly wings tickle the inside of her stomach. When she looked into

the mirror again, the attic's rosy glow had been replaced
by the harsh winking of fluorescent lights.

Heather drew her breath in sharply and glanced
about. She felt like an island in a vast sea of
hardwood flooring. Wooden warm-up
barres stretched across two
mirrored walls.

"Madame Chen, she's
here! She's here!" someone
cried from the doorway.

Heather rubbed at the goose bumps that had erupted
on her arms, despite the studio's warmth. She turned
toward the voice, hoping for another clue about where
here actually was.

"It's *her!*"

"It's Heather Hardin!" The sound of tittering young
voices wafted toward her through the doorway.

Pulling herself up by that imaginary string one of her
ballet teachers always spoke of, Heather crossed the studio
with as much confidence as she could muster. In the hall, a
crowd of costumed dancers applauded her. Standing beside
them, Heather suddenly felt tall and mature.

"Ah! The sleeping beauty awakes at last." A middle-
aged woman with shiny black hair approached Heather
with an outstretched hand. In her left, the woman held a

stick, the kind Heather's ballet teachers always used to correct body positions and tap out rhythms.

"Madame Chen," she guessed aloud, greeting the woman as if she recognized her. "Am I late?"

"Not terribly." Madame Chen smiled. "But you've missed class. And you're not even in makeup yet. Jillian," she said, motioning sharply to a dark-haired girl dressed in a majestic blue queen's robe, "show her the way, will you?"

"Yes, Madame." The girl bowed her head as if the shorter woman were royalty. "Follow me, Heather."

Heather hurried after Jillian, praying that her toe shoes wouldn't echo down the long hall.

Jillian stopped outside a closed door on the right. "I'm so excited to meet you," she bubbled. "When Madame told us you'd agreed to be guest artist . . . well, we all just went crazy at the news. Heather Hardin dancing with the New York City Junior Ballet Ensemble. I mean, it's totally outrageous! And I can't believe you've cut it so close. I mean, just imagine showing up at a dress rehearsal knowing everything!"

"*Everything?*" Heather's voice climbed dangerously.

Jillian narrowed her gaze. "You do know Petipa's choreography, don't you? Act One? 'The Rose Adagio?'"

"Petipa?" Heather repeated, her mind a blank.

Chapter

Four

GUEST
STAR

arius Petipa, the master of the Imperial Russian Ballet? Earth to Heather. You do know his Act One of *The Sleeping Beauty*, don't you?"

"You mean . . . Princess Aurora?" Heather's forced giggle came out more like a snort. "Are you kidding?" She wriggled with excitement. They expected her to be the star, like Aunt Jantina! "I could dance that part in my sleep!" she boasted. It must be true, since they'd invited her here.

Jillian let out a sigh of relief and opened the door to a spacious dressing room. "Where's your dance bag? Didn't you bring any makeup?"

"I was in such a rush . . ."

"Use mine." Jillian opened a boxy case on the mirrored vanity.

Heather touched the tubes and pencils hesitantly, not knowing the first thing about using them. "I'm just so nervous. Look. My hands are shaking. Would you?"

When Jillian smiled, her teeth seemed unusually white against her dark red lipstick. "Sure. I know the feeling. Guess you never get over being nervous no matter how good you are, huh?"

Heather only shrugged. She sank into the nearest chair, letting Jillian drape a plastic cape about her and begin transforming her face into one she barely recognized. "So," Heather said at last, feeling a bit more comfortable now in her role as guest artist, "who's Prince Désiré?"

Jillian frowned. "Are you sure you're feeling all right? You're not jet-lagged or anything?"

"I—I don't think so. Why?"

"We're only doing Act One, remember?" Jillian made

a "tsking" sound with her tongue. "Prince Désiré isn't even *in* it. You should know that."

"And I do. I was just seeing if you did. That's all."

"Testing me, huh?" Grinning at Heather, Jillian stepped back to admire her makeup artistry. "Well, don't worry, Heather. We may be only a lowly *junior* company, but we know our stuff. You won't be disappointed." She whipped the cape off and watched Heather in the mirror. "So, who's partnered you, anyway?"

"Marco Galicia," said Heather promptly, then searched her memory for the name of another of Aunt Jantina's partners, "and, um, Yuri Vasiliev. Those're my favorites, anyway."

"Gosh, and you're so young." Admiration shone in Jillian's blue-shadowed eyes.

A sudden knock on the door startled them both. Before either could reply, a tall, blond dancer wearing an exquisite lavender tutu swept into the room. "You almost ready now? Madame's getting impatient. She wants to run through your solo before the fainting scene, then take it from the top."

"Gosh, Carla," Jillian said, "hello to you, too. You could at least introduce yourself."

The newcomer paused to repin her tiny crown, then turned to admire the delicate wings that were barely wider than her slender waist. "Sorry, hi. Carla Fitch. Gee, you don't look well, Heather." She frowned at Heather's reflection.

Jillian punched Carla's shoulder lightly. "Oh, cut it out. Carla's not only the Lilac Fairy, she's also your understudy, Heather. You look fine. She's just teasing."

"So, what should I tell Madame? Are you coming now or—"

"She still has to warm up," Jillian said. "Give her a break."

"Five minutes, tell her. Ten at the most," Heather said. Jillian and Carla exchanged a look that Heather did not understand. "I'll hurry. And stop looking at me that way. I've warmed up fast lots of times. I know what I'm doing."

"Suit yourself." Carla smirked. "Your loss is my gain."

Fuming at the girl's attitude, Heather brushed past her and Jillian and headed back to the practice room. She heard only a few of Jillian's words— ". . . be fine . . . leave her alone . . ." Then she closed the door.

Spying a pair of leg warmers in the corner by the rosin box, she quickly pulled them on. Surely that would help

her warm up faster. She approached the *barre*, wracking
her brain for the order of those exercises she always did
in class. First, *pliés*—*demi*, then *grands*—in all five
positions. She knew that much. But what came next?

Holding the *barre* with one hand, she hurried through
the basic leg stretches on both sides. Then she tried
some high kicks—*grands battements*. At last she *relevéed en
pointe*, rising to the tips of her hard, wood-toed shoes.
One glance at the elegant line of her body in the mirror
made the pain in her feet suddenly bearable.

Well, here goes, Heather thought, moving to the center of the room. Strains of distant music squeezed under the closed door. She let it catch her and sweep her up as she spun *en pointe* across the floor.

For a final test of her abilities, she tried the dance-run she had attempted in the attic. *Tat-tat-tat-tat-tat.* She stopped, embarrassed.

"Haven't you broken those in yet?" Jillian's voice made Heather jump. The diminutive brunet lifted her long royal gown, breaking character, and rushed toward Heather.

"I—I thought I had."

""Hurry up! Take them off. You can use my hammer."

Heather had no idea what Jillian expected her to do, but she was grateful for the girl's help. She fumbled with the satin ribbons while Jillian fetched the hammer. The slippers finally off, Heather sat in the frog position, amazed at how easily her knees now flopped to the floor.

Jillian returned moments later and flounced down in costume across from Heather. She offered her the hammer, but Heather insisted that Jillian herself do the honors. "Well, I am your mother, Aurora," Jillian teased. "May as well act like it." She began to pound the hard toe boxes in turn. "Don't worry. I'll go easy since we won't have time to wax the insides. Use some extra lamb's wool, maybe. Anyway, it's not like you don't have other pairs you could wear tonight."

Heather nodded, thanked Jillian, and finally managed to retie the toe shoes. "See, Mother?" she joked, terribly pleased with herself. "I can do it all by myself."

"Oh, Heath-er!" Carla's distinctive voice shrilled through the open doorway. "Madame wants you."

"Better go," Jillian whispered. "You don't want to get on her bad side."

Heather tested her turnout one last time in the frog position before springing to her feet. "Coming," she called, and to her great delight, she dance-ran almost soundlessly across the studio and down the long hall toward Madame Chen.

Chapter
Five

TWISTS AND TURNS

eather squinted in the glare of the overhead stage lights, long bars of red, white, and blue bulbs. She tried not to act too surprised by the massive scenery—a wide curving staircase to the rear, castle arches and columns, and transparent curtains painted to resemble forests that stretched to either side.

"Ah, Heather!" Madame Chen's voice rose from some dark place in the auditorium. "Your loyal subjects await." Giggles and titters went out from the front rows. "So. You are ready to work, Carla tells me. Very good. I want to take it from the gift. Where's my Carabosse?"

A dancer made up to look like an old woman wearing a religious habit came sliding onstage from the wings to Heather's right. In her hand she held something that looked like a knitting needle.

"Ah, good. You have the spindle. Kindly present it to Heather here. I want to see her solo before we put it all together. Howie, I think it's about nine-fifty on the tape counter."

"Hey," Carabosse said to Heather, "break a leg, okay?"

"Uh, thanks." What an awful thing to say! And the dancer was smiling, even!

Heather took the needle, traveled downstage, and waited for her music. Her pulse quickened. She just hoped the dance steps would come to her the instant she needed them.

"Play it big now, Heather." Madame's voice seemed to float down from some high, faraway place. "I want to see it from the last row in the balcony, yes?"

All at once, music from hidden speakers boomed like crashing thunder. Heather pretended to prick her finger on the needle, miming her shock and alarm.

"Now, good, and four and five and . . ." The rapping of Madame's dance stick seemed to travel through the auditorium floor right up into Heather's feet. "And hesitate . . . and look at Carabosse . . . and *go!*"

Heather fairly flew upstage to where Queen Jillian was waiting to inspect the injury. Rejecting her mother's concern, Heather—or rather, Princess Aurora—twirled round and round *en pointe*, first playing tipsy, then giddy. Actually dizzy now, it was easy to pretend that the evil fairy Carabosse's spell was fast upon her.

She sank to one knee, then pulled herself up, shrugging off the Queen's alarm. In a series of frenzied *piqué* turns, she circled the stage, bursting at last into a final *grand jeté*. As her right foot landed, a sharp pain riddled her ankle. She collapsed in a heap, her head downstage, one arm extended.

"No, no, Heather! Lengthen. Stretch it out. On your back, dear, feet upstage. Upstage! Let me see it."

Madame's words reached Heather through a fog of pain. She clutched her ankle, biting her bottom lip to keep from crying out.

In an instant, she felt the whoosh of Jillian's robe. "Madame, she's hurt," her new friend called. "I mean it. Come quick!"

The music snapped to a halt. A murmur of voices went out from the darkened front rows. Heather winced as Jillian helped her to sit.

"Did you turn it?" she whispered, as concerned as any real mother would be.

Heather nodded, drawing her right leg up protectively.

Within moments, Madame's pale leather dance slippers appeared from nowhere. Pressing a cold pack to Heather's ankle, she muttered softly in some language Heather didn't understand.

Carla rushed in with a first-aid kit and—Heather couldn't believe it—crutches already. As if the kind and ever-faithful Lilac Fairy knew right where they were and couldn't wait to produce them.

"Aaron! Josh!" Madame squinted into the darkness. "Come up here please. Help get her back to the lounge."

Two young men wearing plumed hats, velvet jackets, and dark boots leaped onstage from the orchestra. They linked arms around Heather and lifted her off the floor.

"What about these?" Carla asked, offering the crutches.

"It's . . . nothing," Heather insisted, avoiding her understudy's eyes. "I'll be fine. Just let me walk it off."

"No." Madame snapped her fingers and set about examining Heather's ankle. "You sit and ice for an hour, and then we will see. Do you want me to wrap it?"

Heather shrugged. "Whatever you think's best."

"So, Carla," said Madame, "are you ready to step in?"

The tall blond nodded earnestly. "I'll go tell my understudy, okay?"

"Fine." Madame looked at her watch and shook her head. "All right, off to the lounge with you, and take the crutches. I will check after we make a first run-through."

Heather nodded, blinking quickly. As embarrassed as she was to be carried off by the boys, she was equally touched by Aaron and Josh's concern for her comfort as they set her gently on the sofa in the lounge.

"Should we give you the rose now, or later?" one teased, referring, Heather assumed, to that famous "Rose Adagio" Jillian had spoken of earlier.

"Later, I hope." She forced a grin. "Thanks."

"Need anything else?" the other boy asked.

"Just a little luck."

The boys fled then, leaving the door ajar and the crutches nearby. Heather eased back on the pillows, fighting tears. She replayed her solo in slow motion, trying to figure out where she'd gone wrong. Maybe it was as simple as a misstep; it could have happened to anyone. Maybe the floor was too slippery. Of course! That had to be it. She should tell Madame. Someone else might get hurt.

Out in the hall she heard voices—one familiar, one not.

"Carla?" She waited for the blond girl to respond. "Tell Madame to check the floor, will you? I think it's super slippery."

"Sure, Heather. Only I doubt it. She had Howie mop it with cola before rehearsal." Carla giggled as their footsteps shuffled off down the hall.

Suddenly, the other girl shrieked. "Five minutes? That's all? You're kidding? Serves her right, then, the fool."

Heather sucked her breath in sharply, as if the very words had slugged her in the stomach.

Chapter
Six

BREAK A LEG!

he dancers' laughter continued to buzz in Heather's ears long after they'd moved on toward the auditorium. At least Carla hadn't tried to take the Princess Aurora costume. Not yet, anyway. Heather shivered at the very thought. She needed it to get home again.

Home. Her thoughts flooded back to the mess of things she'd made with Alison, Megan, and Keisha. If only they were here right now! She could just imagine them, waiting in the wings, watching her dance . . . believing, no, *forgiving* her . . .

She must have slept—must have dreamed about her friends being there, taking care of her—because now, in the drafty lounge, she was clearly alone.

With a great sigh, Heather struggled up to remove the cold pack and examine her ankle. Even through her pink tights, she could see that it was starting to swell. She probed it gently, relieved that the joint was practically numb. If only she were, too.

Sighing again, she eased back against the pillows. Why did she have to act like such a know-it-all? Carla was right. If Heather had warmed up properly, she never would have fallen. What would it have hurt to have asked Jillian or Carla to join her at the *barre*?

Heather knew the answer—her pride. Something her father once said flashed through her mind. "Pride goeth before the fall." She laughed aloud. He had that right.

Strains of Tchaikovsky's *Sleeping Beauty* waltz wove their way to her from the auditorium. The younger dancers would be engaged in the "Garland Dance" now, she knew, weaving designs with hoops and baskets and ropes of flowers. She hated to miss it.

The crutches still lay beside the sofa. Heather decided it couldn't hurt to go watch the ballet from the wings. As she reached for the first crutch, she glimpsed a white basket filled with daisies and pale pink roses on a nearby chair. Snagging the chair leg with the shoulder rest of the crutch, she drew it closer.

A little card was tied to the basket handle. Heather hurried to read it: *Heather, I feel so bad about your fall. Bet it's because I forgot to tell you 'break a leg,' for luck. Feel better soon. Jillian.*

"Omigosh!" Heather's eyes felt hot and itchy. Placing the crutches firmly beneath her arms, she steeled her face in fierce determination and swung off down the hall.

With all the activity of the "Garland Dance" onstage, no one seemed to notice her standing in the wings. Jillian was almost close enough to tap with the tip of one crutch.

"Pssst!" The King turned, and Heather shook her head. "No, Jillian!" Inching closer to the Queen, Heather hunched behind the King and Catalbutte, the royal official, hoping Madame couldn't see her.

Without breaking character, the blue-robed dancer edged toward Heather.

"Thank you for the flowers," she hissed at Jillian. The Queen nodded. Heather licked her lips, working up her courage. "It's not your fault—the accident, I mean. It's mine. I exaggerated a few things. To impress you, I guess."

Jillian turned her head ever so slightly, hiding her

profile with a white feather fan. But she said nothing, just frowned.

"What I said about Marco and Yuri—it's not true. And the fast warm-ups. It was stupid. I was." The final admission locked in her throat. She struggled to release it. "Really, Jillian, I'm not as experienced as you all think."

The corners of Jillian's red lips edged upward ever so slightly. "It doesn't matter. We like you anyway."

"Thanks." She wondered whether her cheeks had gone as pink as her tutu.

"How's your ankle?"

Heather put some weight on it, amazed that it didn't hurt. "I don't know. Okay, maybe. I can't believe it!"

Jillian fanned herself as she replied. "Go to the studio. I'll see if Madame will let me warm you up."

"You'd do that? Really?"

Jillian nodded. "Who knows? Maybe the great Carla will join us. She's not on until the end of the act."

Madame Chen was most generous in releasing Jillian to be with Heather. The Queen shed part of her costume, and worked with Heather for over half an hour to stretch and warm her muscles. Toward the end of the rehearsal Carla joined them, too. She grudgingly admitted that perhaps she'd judged Heather too soon.

48

At last, Heather tested her right ankle *en pointe*. Carla looked on with special interest. "You don't have to do this," she said. "I know your part. The show will go on."

"Honest, it doesn't hurt. I'll be fine," Heather insisted. "At least let me try."

"Come on, then." Jillian grabbed up her robe and slipped it on. "Let's go tell Madame the good news."

By the time Heather reached the stage, however, she was favoring her left leg. Had Carla noticed? Would she tell Madame her good news?

The music stopped abruptly, and the company director's voice boomed from somewhere in the darkened theater. "Heather? Are you there?"

Heather entered from the wings and waved her hand.

"Are you sure you want to try this? Good, then. From your entrance. Howie," she called to the stage manager, "go to three-eighteen, I think."

Heather retreated, awaiting her cue. Queen Jillian, standing just ahead of her on the stage, turned, offering a smile of encouragement. "Break a leg, Heather," she whispered.

Heather bit back a grin. "You, too." In a quiver of violins, she entered, pausing to kiss her stage parents, the Queen and the King.

All at once, a chorus of harp music stole over the

stage, bringing each of four suitors in plumed hats forward to bow in turn to Princess Aurora. So far, so good, Heather thought. This part of the dance was mostly walking and posing. She could handle that.

Then came the spins on her left toe, with her right leg stretching up and out into a *developpé*. From each prince, she accepted a single rose, turning and posing with each presentation. She'd lucked out! That choreographer Petipa seemed to favor the left *pointe*.

But no! As the music swelled, she was compelled to toss the four roses offstage and hold a pose on her right *pointe*. As Prince Josh took her hand, rotating her about in a slow circle, fresh pain shot through her ankle. It wobbled dangerously.

Chapter
Seven

A TOUGH DECISION

eather grimaced, clenching her teeth.

"Are you okay?" Josh whispered.

"Hope so." Her back leg, the one bent into an artistic *attitude*, felt steady enough. If only she could hold her *pointe* through three more rotations, the worst would be over. She hoped.

Josh released her hand to Prince Aaron. His strong support helped her rally. No way was she going to give up. Not when she was so close to taking her bow.

The final two suitors were actually stocky girls, dressed up as young men. Heather supposed it was hard to find enough male dancers this age to fill all the roles.

"Hang in there," her last partner whispered. "Just three pirouettes on your good leg and you're home free."

Heather felt her face melt into a broad smile. With one final glance upstage at Jillian for moral support, she sprang into the closing turns, her heart beating fast. Princess Aurora's stage family was a kaleidoscope of colors as her head swept around, eyes focused only on her spotting point.

The adagio ended in a burst of unexpected applause from the company. Heather sank into a deep curtsy. Tears gathered at the corners of her eyes.

"Brava, Heather! Brava!" Madame Chen's voice rose with emotion.

Heather herself fairly trembled with exhaustion—and relief. Someone pressed a long-stemmed red rose into her hands. It was the Lilac Fairy, Carla, who now led the company in a *reverence*—a group bow—to their guest artist.

Heather swept her arm in an arc that included them all, then returned their applause. She sniffed the rose appreciatively. "Thanks, Carla. But I'll bet you could have danced it just as well."

The blond dancer only shrugged. "Guess we'll never know, will we?"

"Oh, I wouldn't say that." Heather grinned mysteriously. "Will you excuse me? I need to do something in the studio." She couldn't bear to speak to Jillian, though. Good-byes were too hard. Instead, she squeezed the Queen's hand as she went past, then dance-ran as lightly as a fairy down the long tiled hall.

Alone in the light-washed studio, she left a note for Madame Chen and the company, then stood in front of the barre, faced the mirror, and closed her eyes. A wave of dizziness passed through her. Reaching out to steady herself on the wooden rail, her hand brushed only the air.

Heather frowned, opening her eyes. The glow of Ellie's attic welcomed her home. She twirled about, unable to contain her glee. Then, seeing the wide expanse of hardwood floor, she dance-ran from one end of the attic to the other. Was it her imagination, or did the hard toe shoes barely make a sound?

Heather couldn't wait to tell Megan, Alison, and Keisha what had happened—if they were still talking to her, she remembered glumly. Somehow, she just had to get them to at least listen.

Stripping off the tutu and dance shoes, she replaced them exactly where she'd found them and hurriedly dressed. She was halfway down the stairs when she realized she'd forgotten the key and went back for it. Her footsteps echoed throughout the spacious Victorian house.

Ellie met her in the entry hall. The older woman's startlingly blue eyes seemed to dance to the sway of her earrings. "You look positively radiant, Heather." Ellie touched the tip of her silk scarf to each of Heather's cheeks. "As I used to, once upon a time."

Heather's voice rushed out as if she were breathless. "I just danced in *The Sleeping Beauty*. Princess Aurora. Can you believe it?"

"Absolutely. Come! I was just going to have some Mandarin sizzling rice soup. Would you care to join me?"

Heather felt torn. She'd never heard rice sizzle, never tasted a soup with such an interesting name. Better yet, she'd get to spend some time alone with Ellie. The woman had lived such a fascinating life, traveling and performing all over the world. It would take years to hear all her stories. On the other hand, Heather wanted to try to make things right with her friends. She fingered the attic key for a long moment, then slipped it back into the silver box on the table.

"Well?" asked Ellie, gesturing toward the kitchen.

"I'd love to. Really. But I think I'd better go talk to my friends and work things out with them."

Ellie didn't press for details, but something about the sympathetic tilt of her head made Heather pour out the whole embarrassing story. "I don't know why I said those things," she sniffed, feeling miserable all over again. "Everything would have been fine if I hadn't opened my big mouth."

Ellie nudged Heather's hair aside. "Well, dear, we all say things sometimes to impress other people. I've probably stretched my acting credits a bit once or twice, if you want to know the truth."

"Really?" Heather let Ellie lead her into the sitting room, where they eased down onto the long sofa with the carved-face legs. "Did anyone ever find out?"

"Oh, certainly. Truth has a way of catching up with you. The surprising thing is, those people would have hired me on my audition alone. I never needed to embellish at all."

Heather sighed, thinking of her friends. What would happen when they found out the truth? Reaching over, she hugged the

58

slightly plump woman. The scent of roses clung to the teacher's skin. "Thanks, Ellie. You always know just the right thing to say."

Ellie retucked a silvery wisp that had strayed from her handsome French twist. "Glad you think so, dear. Eh, *bien*. I can see you've one foot out the door."

Heather laughed. "I just wish I knew what to do first!"

"Start with the easiest and go from there."

"That's just what Mom always says."

Ellie simply shrugged.

Thinking of the grand adventure she'd just had in the attic, Heather hurried out the front door and down the shoveled walk. She paused near Alison's house. The mini-blinds in the kitchen were angled, making it hard to see exactly who was seated around the table. Was it her friends? At the thought of them watching her leave Ellie's and not even coming out, Heather swallowed hard.

All at once, she knew what she had to do.

Chapter

Eight

PROMISES
TO KEEP

s Heather and her mother made their way toward Metro Civic Center's stage, a strange shiver of recognition passed through her. From the castle columns and arches to the wide curving staircase and gloomy forest, the set for Aunt Jantina's *Sleeping Beauty* ballet looked exactly like the junior company's. Judging from the way Aunt Jantina lay sprawled on the floor, Heather realized that they were rehearsing Act One. She recognized that evil fairy Carabosse, even though the

old woman had just whipped off her religious habit, revealing a clown-red wig. Heather jumped when, without warning, Carabosse disappeared through a trap door in a puff of smoke.

"Mom, did you see that? Wasn't it fantastic?"

Mrs. Hardin nodded and touched her fingers to her lips. "Here comes the Lilac Fairy. I think this part's almost over. They should be carrying Jantina off soon. Maybe we can catch her backstage."

Heather followed her mother through the darkened auditorium, up some stairs, and into the wings. After clearing their presence with some official-looking man, they waited for Aunt Jantina.

When the six court noblemen finally set Princess Aurora down backstage, Heather raced toward her, waving her hand. Aunt Jantina looked startled but pleased to see her. And though Heather was dying to tell the dancer about her own experiences as the Sleeping Beauty, she held her tongue. Time was short, and Heather needed to ask her something very important.

Aunt Jantina air-kissed Mrs. Hardin's cheek and tweaked Heather's nose. "So what brings you here? Can't wait for the real thing?"

Mrs. Hardin gestured for Heather to reply. Aunt Jantina leaned closer. "Remember when I called you this morning and asked for extra tickets?" began Heather. Aunt Jantina nodded, and she pressed on. "I kind of promised my friends too soon and, well . . ." She glanced back at her mom for moral support. "See, I made up all this stuff to impress them, only it didn't and now they're mad at me."

Aunt Jantina offered a sympathetic smile. "How can I help?"

"I was hoping you'd come over tomorrow for breakfast—before you take class, I mean."

"Don't tell me. Let me guess. Your friends will be there, too."

"If I'm lucky."

Jantina glanced at Heather's mother. "Make it something light. And if I'm lucky, I'll have a surprise for you."

Heather's heart pounded almost as loudly as her fist on Alison's front door. At last Alison herself opened it. "Oh, hi, Heather," she said, avoiding Heather's eyes.

Heather shifted her weight from one foot to the other. "Are Megan and Keisha here, too? I really need to talk to you guys. All day I've been feeling so awful."

Alison nodded glumly and stepped aside, taking Heather's coat. "They're in my room. Come on back."

Alison's twin brothers flew past them in the hallway. She closed her door behind Heather. Megan and Keisha glanced up from the jigsaw puzzle they were working on Alison's white wicker desk. They squirmed and looked at each other, as if they didn't know quite what to say.

"I—I don't blame you all for being mad at me," began Heather, trying not to fidget with her fingers. "Guess I really acted like a jerk, making up all that stuff, acting like I was such a great dancer. I—I wanted to impress you, but maybe, well . . ."

"No need to," Megan said gently. "And we're not mad. Really."

"More like embarrassed for you," Alison chimed in. "We just didn't know what to say."

Keisha opened her mouth as if to add something more, but Heather shook her head. It was easier, somehow, when she thought they were mad at her. She wished they wouldn't let her off so easily. "Just let me finish, okay? Let me say how sorry I am. I—I've been so afraid you wouldn't ever want to talk to me again and—"

"Of course we want to talk to you," Alison interrupted. "How else are we going to find out what happened in the attic today? You did go there, didn't you?"

Something melted, finally, inside Heather and made her grin. "I'll tell you everything. That's the rule. Only promise you'll all come tomorrow for breakfast. So you can meet Aunt Jantina."

Megan pressed back a giggle and rolled her eyes. "Oh, no, Heather. You're doing it again!"

"I'm not," Heather promised. "She'll be there."

And with that, all the girls stacked hands, palms down, and shouted, "All for one and one for all!" promising to be there at nine sharp.

The next day they arrived right on schedule. Heather only wished she could say the same for Aunt Jantina. By the time the girls had milked every last detail of her adventure through the mirror, they were beginning to make throat-clearing noises and glance at the clock.

"Honest, she'll be here," said Heather, though she

herself was beginning to have doubts.

Alison cast the others a "here we go again" look.

Heather stared hard at the door as if her sheer will could make the bell ring. After several long, awkward minutes, she got up to get the girls' coats from the closet. "I—I don't know what to say. Aunt Jantina promised. My mom can tell you so herself."

"That's okay," said Megan. "I've got to go write up your adventure in our notebook anyway."

Heather opened the door, sighing in frustration. A uniformed messenger was standing there, about to knock. "Delivery for Miss Heather Hardin."

"I'm Heather." Her rushed signature on line eleven looked like a stranger's. "Thanks."

The girls crowded closer as she tore the envelope open.

"What does it say? Read it!" Keisha urged.

Heather's hand trembled with excitement as she held Aunt Jantina's fancy stationery up for their inspection. "Girls, don't blame Heather for this one," she read. "I'm running late again—so what else is new?—but I wanted you to have these backstage passes for

opening night. Maybe Jenna has a friend who can use Heather's seat. See you soon! Kiss, kiss."

"Kiss, kiss!" Alison, Megan, and Keisha chorused, throwing their arms around each other—and around Heather, too. Then, all together, they jumped and squealed as one.

Diary

Dear Diary,

Me and my big mouth! If I've learned one thing today, it's not to exaggerate and pretend you know more than you really do. Going to Ellie's attic and being a ballet star helped me realize that.

Did you know that stages are built on a slant? I sure didn't, until my piqué turns. Going downstage made me go faster and faster as I headed toward the audience! And toe shoes look pretty, but believe me, they're really uncomfortable. The padding doesn't help much. Your toes blister and bleed, just so you can hold a pose for a few seconds. Jillian had lots of blisters, and I would, too, if I danced as much as she does.

It was so cool how Keisha, Megan, Alison, and I got to watch Aunt Jantina's ballet from backstage. All the dancers look so different up close. We peeked out during the final bows and waved to my family in the front row.

Maybe someday I'll go back to the attic and try that tutu on again!

Luv,

Heather